CYBER_Sleuths
The Super Berries Scam

BY NATASHA DEEN

ILLUSTRATED
BY MARIANO EPELBAUM

STONE ARCH BOOKS
a capstone imprint

Published by Stone Arch Books, an imprint of Capstone.
1710 Roe Crest Drive, North Mankato, Minnesota 56003
capstonepub.com

Copyright © 2025 by Capstone. All rights reserved. No part of this publication may be reproduced in whole or in part, or stored in a retrieval system, or transmitted in any form or by any means, electronic, mechanical, photocopying, recording, or otherwise, without written permission of the publisher.

Library of Congress Cataloging-in-Publication Data is available on the Library of Congress website.

ISBN: 9781669075202 (hardcover)
ISBN: 9781669075271 (paperback)
ISBN: 9781669075479 (ebook PDF)

Summary: Dalia Gopie is shorter than all her friends. Then she discovers that her favorite social media influencer is promoting a miracle fruit—one that guarantees to make anyone taller overnight! Is this online fad the real deal, or is the popular influencer selling a tall tale? With the help of other Cyber Sleuths—a network of mystery-solving kids—and legit online resources, Dalia uncovers the truth about this too-good-to-be-true product.

Designer: Kay Fraser

This book is published in partnership with the International Society for Technology in Education (ISTE).

Any additional websites and resources referenced in this book are not maintained, authorized, or sponsored by Capstone. All product and company names are trademarks™ or registered® trademarks of their respective holders.

TABLE OF CONTENTS

CHAPTER ONE
SHORT FRY.................5

CHAPTER TWO
IT'S A MIRACLE..............12

CHAPTER THREE
GETTING THE BERRIES.........16

CHAPTER FOUR
THIS IS "BERRY" BAD..........21

CHAPTER FIVE
THIS CAN'T BE HAPPENING......30

CHAPTER SIX
BACK TO THE STORE...........34

CHAPTER SEVEN
THINGS AREN'T WHAT THEY SEEM...40

CHAPTER EIGHT
THE RESEARCH BEGINS.........46

CHAPTER NINE
UNRAVELING THE TRUTH........54

CHAPTER TEN
THIS IS "BERRY" GOOD.........62

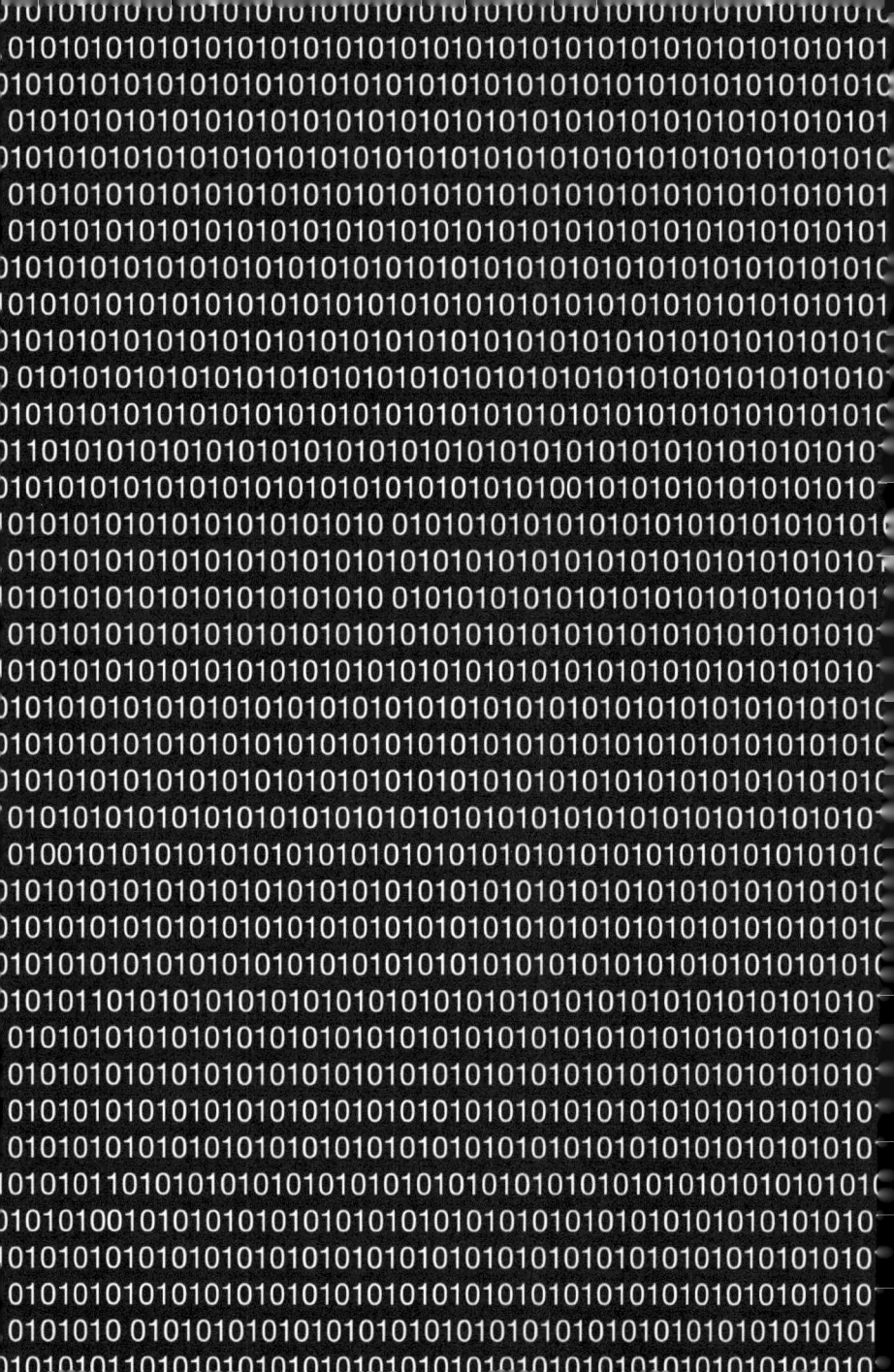

CHAPTER ONE

SHORT FRY

Dalia Gopie flopped on her bed and groaned. What an epic failure the last hour had been. She'd met up with her friends. It was supposed to be an awesome lunch because everyone had been so busy throughout the summer, and they hadn't seen each other since forever. This was their chance to catch up before school started next week.

Except . . . except, over the summer, everyone had grown. Everyone but Dalia. All her friends looked older, more mature. Now Dalia was the shortest and youngest looking; she felt like the little sister who tags along with her older siblings. It would have been OK, sort of, except when they went to their favorite hang-out to eat. The waitress tried to give Dalia the kids' menu. That was for kids who were 10 or younger! Adding to the humiliation, her friends piled on with the teasing. Sick of being called "Short Fry," Dalia had pretended she got a call to head home.

Everyone looks like they belong in middle school, except me, she thought. She looked in the mirror. Before lunch, she thought she'd looked good. Now, she looked like a baby. *I bet everyone at school will look grown-up, except me. What if*—she pushed the thought from her head, but her brain filled in the last part. *What if I look so young that my friends don't want to hang out with me anymore?*

The buzz of her phone startled her. When she saw it was her best friend, Nils, she answered the video call.

He appeared on the screen. Nils must have biked home because his cheeks were red and strands of his blond hair were plastered to his forehead. "We teased you too hard," he said as soon as he saw her. "By the time we realized you weren't laughing along, you were already gone. I'm sending you something from the group."

Dalia checked her text. It was a picture of her friends, holding a sign that said, "Our bad! So sorry!"

"That's cool," she said. "Thanks." Dalia grinned. "I like the silver glitter on the sign."

"What happened?" he asked. "Normally, you're cool when we roast you."

"That was when we were all close in height and stuff," said Dalia. "Now, you guys look grown-up, and I look like a little kid—"

"Oh, man, no wonder you didn't laugh," Nils said.

"Dalia! I'm home! Come help with the groceries, please," Mom's voice rang up the stairs.

"I gotta go," said Dalia.

Nils laughed. "I heard. Say hi to your mom. We'll talk later?"

"You got it." Dalia ended the call and headed downstairs.

"Hey, pumpkin. How was your day? Was it great to see your friends?" Mom reached into a cloth bag and pulled out a jar of tomato sauce.

"It was . . . OK," she said. She told her mom about how much older everyone looked and how embarrassing it was to get the little kids' menu.

Mom laughed. "Trust me, there'll be a day you'll be thrilled when people think you're young." She cupped Dalia's chin. "It's frustrating, but we all grow at our own pace, honey. You'll catch up with your friends soon enough."

"That's such a mom answer," Dalia said as she put the milk in the fridge.

"You may look young," Mom said, "but you're getting older. If you weren't maturing into a fine young lady—"

Dalia groaned. "Fine young lady?"

"We wouldn't allow you to go on social media, would we?"

"Yeah, but you still have a ton of rules about it," Dalia complained.

"To protect you," Mom said. "With school starting up, maybe now's a good time to review those rules again—"

Dalia sighed. "No posting photos or videos of my face, my account has to be private, and I can only make connections with people I know in real life." Dalia ticked off the rules on her fingers.

After they were done unpacking, Dalia headed to her room and opened one of her favorite social media apps, Clik-Clok. As a video started playing, excitement shot through her veins. Mom may not have been able to help her, but this video might be the answer to her problems.

CHAPTER TWO

IT'S A MIRACLE

Janeese, one of the influencers Dalia followed, had posted a video. Dalia hit refresh and the clip played again.

"Now, you know I never think of you guys as my audience," Janeese said as she flipped back her blond hair. "You're more than my friends. You're my family, and you know I always have your back when it comes to great products, right?"

Dalia leaned forward.

Janeese held up a white bowl full of black-colored berries. "These are aronia berries," she said, "and they're my fave food." She plucked one from the bowl and brought it close to the camera. It was small, almost like a blueberry, but darker in color. Under the lights of her studio, the berry seemed to glow.

"This little berry is a superfruit," she said. "And it's the key to living forever." Janeese grinned and winked. "OK, not exactly. But these berries are packed with vitamin C, which helps protect our bodies from free radicals. They've got tons of fiber, carbs, and manganese. But my friends, this tiny berry is so much more." Janeese gently placed the berry in the center of her palm. "Aronia berries are full of antioxidants, folate, iron—and you know what these are great for? Growing

tall! Seriously, you guys, these berries are like magic! It's not exactly overnight," said the influencer, "but pretty close! You won't believe it, but I actually grew an inch in a couple of days! I buy Alto Farms aronia berries, but these bad boys are selling out quickly. Pick up a batch of these little beauties before they're gone!" She placed the berry back into the bowl and the clip ended.

An inch in a couple of days? Amazing! If I had those berries, I'd be two or three inches taller by the time school starts, Dalia thought. *And if I keep up with it, I'll be taller than my friends by the end of the month . . .*

Then excitement turned to anxiety. *What did Janeese say about the berries selling out?* Dalia hopped off the bed. She had to get the fruit before it was too late.

CHAPTER THREE

GETTING THE BERRIES

Dalia texted Nils. **Heading to the grocery store. Wanna come?**

Three dots appeared on the screen, then, **Yeah! Be at your house in 10!**

Dalia rushed downstairs. "Heading out with Nils to the store!" she called to her mom.

"OK, have fun!" Mom called back.

Dalia paced the sidewalk. *What's taking him so long?* When Nils's bike came into view, Dalia exhaled impatiently.

"I thought you said ten minutes," she said, strapping on her helmet.

Nils blinked and checked his watch. "I'm on time."

"Never mind, let's go," said Dalia, "before it's too late!" She jumped on her skateboard and started down the sidewalk.

Nils followed along on his bike. "What are we rushing for?" he asked.

Dalia told him about the berries.

Nils slowed. His eyebrows pulled together. "Berries can make you grow that fast?"

Dalia really wanted to get to the store, but she could hear the doubt in Nils's voice. There was one way to erase his worries. "Here, I'll show you." Dalia took out her phone and showed him Janeese's clip.

Instead of nodding, though, Nils frowned.

"Do you think that's actually true?"

Dalia shrugged. "I'm not sure, but I have to try, right?"

"Do you, though?" asked Nils. "You look fine to me."

Dalia rolled her eyes. "OK, Dad."

Nils held up his hands. "OK, OK."

Dalia often helped her parents with the grocery shopping, so she knew where the produce section was. She beelined toward the fruits when they walked into the store.

"Where are they? Where are they?" she muttered. Finally, Dalia spotted the berries. She stared at the price. *Wow,* she thought, *these are more expensive than I imagined.*

"Whoa! Those are pricey!" said Nils, peeking over her shoulder.

"I was thinking the same thing," Dalia

said. Indecision wriggled in her stomach. Maybe they were *too* expensive. But then she thought of walking the halls as the shortest kid in the school. And then she thought of her friends calling her "Short Fry." Dalia picked up a basket and went to the checkout.

"Wanna head back to my house?" Nils asked. "My dad's home, so we can hang out in the pool."

But Dalia was too excited to try the fruit. "Tomorrow, OK? Come over super early and we'll hang for the whole day," she said.

Nils waved as Dalia raced home. As soon as she was inside, she washed the fruit. In just seven days, she was going to grow! Maybe she'd even be taller than her friends. *We'll see who the short fry is at the end of the month,* she thought. She popped a handful of berries into her mouth. But as soon as she started chewing, she began to choke.

CHAPTER FOUR

THIS IS "BERRY" BAD

The berries tasted awful. They were sour, and it felt like they were turning her mouth to cement as she chewed. Dalia forced herself to swallow, then chugged a glass of water, trying to get the taste out.

"Wow, what's going on?" Sanaa, Dalia's older sister, asked as she came into the kitchen. She pushed her hair behind her ear and sat at the counter.

"These berries. They're terrible." Dalia took another swig of water.

Sanaa laughed. "And colorful. Look at your face!"

Dalia opened her camera app and groaned. The berries had turned her mouth bright blue. She definitely wouldn't be eating these before school!

"Why are you gorging on these berries, anyway?" Sanaa took one and sniffed it.

"Oh, I just thought I'd eat some fruit." Dalia shrugged. It wasn't a lie, exactly. Trying to explain to Sanaa that she was following a Clik-Clok trend was sure to cause a Big Sister lecture.

"Save room for dinner." Sanaa raised her eyebrows. "You're helping me, remember? Taco night."

Dalia nodded. "Yeah, of course. I'll be down in a bit to help." She escaped to her room, then scrolled to Janeese's account. *How did Janeese manage to eat those berries without gagging?* She wondered. Dalia loaded the video and watched again. Janeese held up the bowl of berries, then put one in the palm of her hand. When she was done talking, she returned the berry to the bowl. She never actually ate any. *That's funny,* Dalia thought. *I could have sworn she had eaten some.* Dalia turned her attention to the comments section. *I wonder what other people thought when they ate the berries.*

ACK! Are they supposed to be THIS sour? asked user @fruit4life67.

Dalia laughed. *At least it wasn't just me!*

Add them to a smoothie, suggested user @palmdesertgrrl.

User @sunsetsandpitties said, **Mix them into**

your juice or smoosh them into your yogurt.

But as she continued reading, impatience made Dalia's shoulders slump.

These berries are a miracle! gushed user @Mattbox283. **They def help you grow! I noticed a difference the next day!**

Forget the next day! I swear I gained an inch the SAME day! claimed @phillyjeffdaxter.

Totally! agreed user @jumpin2life. **I'm amazed by the results. Three inches in a week!**

The comments went on and on.

These are my go-to fruit from now on! posted @stephaniesmith45.

I can't get over how fast I grew! @john34milner's comment followed that one.

Dalia scrolled through more comments, then returned to Janeese's main feed to search for the smoothie recipe.

Janeese's smiling face beamed from her most recent video. She was in her white kitchen with a basket of the berries on the counter.

Dalia hit play.

"Hey, my friends." Janeese wiggled her fingers at the camera. "So, I'm getting a lot of feedback and questions about these berries. I love, love, love how positive everyone's experiences have been! A little bit more info—researchers are finding all kinds of amazing things about our favorite berry. It's making waves for its anti-cancer properties and how it helps keep your skin clear and healthy!"

Dalia's phone pinged. It was Nils. **I was online and didn't see anything about your berries having magical growing properties. But I did find someone called @CyberSleuth14.**

Did they try the berries? Did it work for them? Dalia texted back.

No, texted Nils, **but remember the videos that were going around about Bigfoot in the park? @CyberSleuth14 was the one who posted evidence that it was a hoax.**

Dalia's eyebrows pulled together. **What does that have to do with berries?**

Three dots appeared on her screen as Nils texted back. **The cryptid claim was kind of unbelievable . . . kind of like Janeese's claims about the berries. Maybe you should take a look at @CyberSleuth14's video.**

Dalia puffed out an exasperated breath. **Cryptids are nothing like berries! For one thing, cryptids don't exist. These berries do!**

I'm not saying it's the same thing, Nils texted. **But berries that make you grow a**

couple of inches in a day sound fake. Just like the cryptid. CyberSleuth14 used a hashtag—#cyber_sleuth_truth—you should look at his videos.

Exasperation turned to annoyance. Why was Nils being like this? All Dalia wanted to do was grow a bit. As her friend, she felt that Nils should have supported her. Dalia ignored his text and went back to Janeese's video.

"Now—" Janeese moved to a blender on her counter. "—I know they can be tart. So, I'm going to show you how to make an amazing smoothie. I use organic honey to offset the sour taste . . ."

Dalia wrote down the recipe. Then she hurried downstairs to try making the drink.

"Good, you're here," said Sanaa. "I thought you'd forgotten about dinner."

"What? No, of course not." Dalia tucked

her phone in her pocket. *Tomorrow,* she thought. *As soon as I get up, I'm making a smoothie.* Nothing would stop her from using the power of those berries to get taller.

Later that night, Nils sent another text. **Did you try the berries? Did it work?**

Dalia turned her phone to mute and went to bed.

CHAPTER FIVE

THIS CAN'T BE HAPPENING

The next morning, Dalia raced to the kitchen to make her smoothie. She opened the fridge and stared in disbelief. Her berries were gone!

"Did someone move my fruit?" she called up the stairs.

Her dad appeared at the top of the staircase. "I used them," he said, putting on his glasses, and walking down to meet her.

"What?" Dalia's voice was sharp. "Why did you take them?"

Dad's eyebrows went up at the question. "Your sister said you bought them but found the berries too sour. I thought I'd make it into a pie." He reached into the fridge and pulled it out. "Now, it's sweet enough to eat."

"How could you do that!" Dalia struggled not to shout. "They were mine!"

The commotion brought Sanaa and Mom running into the kitchen.

"I'm sorry," Dad said, hurt. "I thought you'd like the surprise."

"I don't," Dalia said. "Now I have to buy another basket. You shouldn't touch my stuff without asking." She stalked to her room.

Sanaa followed. "What is wrong with you?"

"Nothing, but it's my food—" Dalia started to say.

"It's *not* your food," Sanaa corrected her. "It's *our* food. We share in this family."

"Not always." Dalia folded her arms. "Those were mine, and they have to be eaten fresh. That's what the video said! Now I have to go to the store again."

"Fine," said Sanaa, looking confused. "While you're there, you can replace *my* yogurt that you ate and *Dad's* ice cream that you also ate. Oh, and *Mom's* apples."

"That's not fair!" Heat rose from Dalia's neck to her face.

"If you're going to get mad at Dad for doing something nice for you, and if you're going to get possessive over food, then it's definitely fair." Sanaa headed up the stairs.

CHAPTER SIX

BACK TO THE STORE

Seething from losing her berries and from her sister's demands, Dalia got dressed to leave. She stormed out the front door and almost slammed into Nils.

"What are you doing here?" she asked.

His eyes widened. "You invited me over. You said come early so we can hang all day."

Dalia groaned. "I'm sorry. I forgot—I have to go to the grocery store."

"Again?" Nils asked with a shrug. "I'll come along. We can hang after." As they headed out, he asked, "Did you try those berries?"

"No. That's why I'm going back to the store." Dalia told him about her dad making a pie from her berries.

"That's awesome," said Nils. "Your dad is an amazing baker. I can't wait to try a piece!"

"That's not the point!" Dalia rounded on him. "He took my food without asking."

Nils looked confused. "So? I've never known anyone in your family to have to ask about food."

"That's—never mind." Dalia sped to the store, leaving Nils rushing to keep up. They didn't talk for the rest of the trip, but she noticed Nils occasionally glancing at her with concern on his face.

Once in the grocery store, Dalia raced to get her berries. She reached for the last basket at the same time as a short teenage boy.

"Those are mine," she said, refusing to let go.

"I got here first," he said, flipping his black hair off his eyes, "but there's no problem. We can split the cost and the berries."

"No, I need all of them!" She wrenched the basket from his grip, then remembered to grab the other items Sanaa had told her to buy. When Dalia got to the checkout, she turned to Nils to complain about the teen, but Nils was gone.

She finished paying and headed outside. Nils was waiting by the entrance.

"Where did you go?" asked Dalia.

"I went to apologize to that guy," he said tightly. "You were super rude."

"I wasn't—" Dalia protested. "He was going to take the last basket. I was there first!"

Nils shook his head in disgust. "No, you weren't. I was there, and I saw what happened. He got to the berries first. And he was going to share! Geez, Dalia, what is going on with you?" He pointed at her cloth bag. "You're weirdly obsessed with these berries, and it's not cool."

"It's totally cool," said Dalia. "These berries are going to help me grow! If I eat them, I'll be way taller when school starts next week."

"They're fruit, Dalia," said Nils. "They can't give you super abilities like growing fast. Did you even look at that hashtag I told you about?"

"No, not yet. But the berries work. There's research and Janeese said—"

Nils scoffed. "Yeah, research . . . "

"You don't get it—" Dalia's temper was rising, and she could feel the blood rushing in her ears.

"You're right," Nils said. "I don't get it. My best friend wouldn't forget about hanging out with me, she wouldn't ignore my texts, she wouldn't get mad at her dad for making some gross berries into something actually good, and she definitely wouldn't get into a fight with some random guy over fruit!" He turned to leave.

"Wait—what about hanging out at my house?" Dalia called after him.

"Hang with your berries," he said. "You obviously care way more about them than anything else." Nils stalked away, and Dalia was alone on the sidewalk.

CHAPTER SEVEN

THINGS AREN'T WHAT THEY SEEM

When Dalia got home, she put away the groceries, then headed to her room.

Sorry about forgetting to hang out, she texted Nils, **but I'm not wrong about the berries.**

After a few seconds, the dots appeared. **Thanks for the apology,** he texted back. **I found another video from someone called @RhysCybersleuth and they posted a video about how you can't believe everything you read online.**

I know that! "Honestly," she mumbled as she texted. **I'M NOT A BABY.**

Nils's text came back immediately. **But you believe Janeese without any proof!**

Dalia jabbed at the screen's keyboard. **She is backed by research!**

WHAT research? Nils texted.

I'll prove it to Nils, Dalia thought as she opened her app. *I'll find the proof and show him that he's wrong.* She scrolled to Janeese's feed and to the post where the influencer talked about the research on the berries.

That's funny, Dalia thought as she scrolled through the comments, *I could have sworn Janeese mentioned details about the research.* But she wasn't finding any. As she kept scrolling, Dalia realized that while Janeese mentioned "research" in a few of her posts, she never said anything specific about it.

"Done with your temper tantrum?" Sanaa stood in Dalia's doorway, her arms crossed in front of her chest.

"I—she said the berries would make me grow really fast, like a few inches in a few days," said Dalia, confused. "She said there was research to prove it."

Sanaa's arms dropped to her side. "Who said that about the berries?"

"When I saw my friends last week, they were all bigger than me. Like, really bigger. And they kept calling me 'Short Fry.'" Dalia held out her phone to Sanaa. "Janeese said these berries were a miracle food. That they'd make me grow."

"Berries are an awesome food." Sanaa joined her on the bed. "And they're great for lots of things, liking making sure a person has proper nutrition to help them grow. But nothing can make you grow *that* fast."

"But she said . . ." Dalia scrolled through the feed, hoping to find something to convince her sister.

Sanaa tilted her head. "Wait. Have you been acting so weird because you're trying to get taller?"

Dalia shrugged and looked away.

Sanaa hugged Dalia. "Everyone in this family is pretty tall. You'll catch up."

"That's what Mom said." Dalia fiddled with the phone. "But what if I don't grow?"

"You'll be great no matter what size you are." Then Sanaa pointed to the image of a smiling Janeese. "If I were you, I'd be more worried about the things she's saying. It doesn't sound like she's telling the whole truth."

"No, she's telling the truth," Dalia said. "I just haven't found the video where she talks about the research."

"If there's proof, wouldn't she mention it on every post?" Sanaa asked.

"Maybe there's a time limit to the video," Dalia said defensively. "You're wrong. I'm going to find the evidence to show the berries help you grow."

"Then I look forward to you proving me wrong." Sanaa gave Dalia a final hug, then left.

Dalia stared at Janeese's feed. Why would the influencer lie? *She wouldn't*, thought Dalia. *I just have to work harder to find the proof.* Determined to show both Nils and Sanaa they were wrong, Dalia kept searching.

CHAPTER EIGHT

THE RESEARCH BEGINS

"Dalia!" Mom called up the stairs. "Dinner!"

Dalia set down her phone and rubbed her eyes. She'd been searching Janeese's feed for over 40 minutes and still hadn't found the research video.

She went to the kitchen. Before dinner began, Dalia apologized to her dad. After dinner, she helped with the cleanup, then took her favorite spot in the living room's battered recliner. She sank into the worn cushions and opened her phone.

Maybe Janeese talked about the research a while ago, she thought. *What I need to do is start at the beginning of her posts, then work my way to the most recent videos.*

Dalia settled in and started reading.

"Are you still on your phone?" Mom came into the room. She held out a plate of apple slices. "I don't like you being online for so long."

"It's not—I'm doing homework," said Dalia.

"Homework?" Mom asked, surprised. "School doesn't start for another week."

"It's not for school." Her face turning red with embarrassment, Dalia told her mom about her plan to use the berries to grow.

Mom's mouth formed an 'O.' "Honey, fruit

can't make you grow that fast."

"But Janeese said there's research," Dalia chewed on the apple and returned to scrolling.

"Have you found any proof?" Mom asked gently.

"No . . . but there must be some, right? She wouldn't lie, would she? I'm looking for proof, but it's really annoying." Dalia held up her phone. "Every time I open a new feed, the old screen gets hidden. I hate having to go back and forth."

Mom patted her leg. "Come with me."

They headed to the family desktop. Mom opened Clik-Clok on the computer's browser.

Dalia stood beside her and brought up Janeese's feed. "Now what?"

"See this hashtag, fruit4life? Watch what I do." Mom pressed down on the control key, then clicked the mouse. "This will open the link in a tab next to the original website. Now, I can click and drag the tab to an empty spot on the screen." Mom did this. "Now, they're side by side and I can look at them at the same time. Which means it's much easier to compare everything." Mom leaned into the screen. "Do you see any research hashtags?"

Dalia scanned, then shook her head. "No."

"Then let's look online for the proof. What kind of berries are you eating?"

"Aronia berries," Dalia typed the term into the search engine.

"Let's add 'benefits' to your search," Mom said. "Then we can compare what Janeese said to what other sources say."

After the page loaded, Mom said, "You want to study the websites. Look for ones that are reputable. Are they government sites?

Or medical sites? Those will be more trustworthy than a random person who creates on online account and posts a blog. Traditional newspapers are also good because the journalists have to validate their sources. Do you know what that means?"

Dalia shook her head.

"It means they must double-check any source they use for their information. So that if someone wants to check the facts, they can do so." Mom nudged Dalia's shoulder. "Like we're doing right now." She squeezed Dalia's arm, then left her to do the research.

Half an hour in, Dalia realized that Janeese was right—sort of. There were benefits to eating the berries, but Janeese's claims that they would help Dalia grow an inch in a week were definitely not true. None of the sources Dalia checked agreed with Janeese. They all said that while the berries are great for making sure a person gets proper nutrients, which might help them grow, genetics was a big contributor to a person's height. Dalia shifted in her seat. She'd solved part of the mystery—the berries were good for people, but they didn't perform miracles.

A hollow, heavy feeling replaced the determination Dalia had been feeling. Maybe Janeese hadn't been totally lying when she posted those videos about the berries, but she hadn't exactly told the whole truth. Eating the berries wouldn't make Dalia grow a few inches in a few days. The realization made Dalia feel like a fool. She'd believed Janeese, and she'd fought with Sanaa, her dad, and Nils over it. That felt even worse than knowing she'd be the shortest kid in school this year. But there was still a question sounding in Dalia's ears. *Why would Janeese have exaggerated the benefits of the fruit?*

CHAPTER NINE

UNRAVELING THE TRUTH

The next day, as Dalia sat on the couch and continued scrolling through Janeese's feed, she realized something else. No matter which fruit Janeese highlighted, she used the same words to describe it.

"Miracle, superpower," Dalia muttered to herself. "Not every fruit can be a miracle."

"Are you talking to yourself?" Sanaa ruffled Dalia's hair.

"Look at this." She showed her sister what she'd discovered. "Every time Janeese talks about a new food, it's her favorite food and it's life-changing. But not everything can be that important, right?"

"Right," said Sanaa. "But if she hypes things, then you get hyped."

Dalia sat back. She never thought of that, but the more she thought, the more she realized her sister was right. When Janeese got excited and used words like "miracle" and "guaranteed," it made Dalia believe her posts were true.

Dalia groaned and put her head on Sanaa's shoulder. "The first time I saw the video, I remember thinking it was too good to be true."

"It's OK," said Sanaa, hugging her sister. "You wanted to be tall like your buddies, that's all."

"Maybe," said Dalia, "but it feels like more. When I saw her video, it made me feel so excited. And the more I got excited, the more of her stuff I watched and believed."

"So, then, the more her stuff trends and the bigger her account becomes," said Sanaa. "It's part of an influencer's business plan. Instead of beating yourself up for getting fooled, you should be proud of yourself for seeing the truth."

"Maybe." Dalia kept scrolling. But this time, she wasn't looking for information. She was checking to see how each post made her feel. After a few minutes, Dalia set down her phone. Some of the posts made her happy, but others—like the ones that tell her that she should be taller and that she was doing something wrong if the berries don't work for her like Janeese said they did—made her feel anxious.

Dalia texted Nils. **You were—** She stopped. Some things needed to be said in person. "Mom!" Dalia went into the kitchen. "Is it cool if I go to Nils's house?"

Mom nodded. "Be back for dinner, OK?"

Before she left, Dalia packed a couple of slices of Dad's pie. When she got to Nils's house, she took a deep breath and tried to calm the squiggly feeling inside her. She rang the bell.

Nils answered.

"Hey," she said. "I owe you pie. And an apology."

Nils took the pie and stepped aside. "Come in."

Dalia and Nils headed to the kitchen. Over a slice of dessert, she told him about the berries and what she'd uncovered about Janeese's claims. "I feel silly," she said. "I just bought into everything she said without verifying the information myself. And I acted like a total jerk to you and everyone else. I'm really sorry."

"Thanks," said Nils. "I accept your apology." Nils served them another slice of pie. "Does it really bug you that everyone in our group is taller?"

"No. Yes. No—it's—" Dalia took a breath. "It just felt like everyone was bigger and more mature. It made me worry that maybe we wouldn't be friends, you know? Because I look younger than everyone else and maybe you'll think I'm too babyish to hang with."

Nils hugged her. "Dalia, you're the best person I know. You're amazing on a skateboard and you're a great friend—no matter how tall or short you are."

Dalia hugged him back. "Thanks. I needed

that." She took a bite of the pie. "There's something I don't get. Why did Janeese exaggerate what the berries could do?"

Nils took out his phone. "Remember the cybersleuth I was telling you about? I found someone else. Her handle is @cybersleuthchyenne. Look at this video." Nils found the post and hit play.

A girl about their age with two black braids came on the screen. "Hey friends, Chyenne here." She waved. "Did you know that sometimes companies pay influencers to review or promote their products? When that happens, an influencer is supposed to tell you. There are a few ways they can do this. They can tell you in the video or the image, or they can use a hashtag. Some examples might be #ad or #sponsored. But some influencers aren't clear about their partnerships, and they may

use hashtags like #collab or #promo. That's not cool—if they're getting paid, they should tell you."

Nils paused the video. "Did Janeese have any hashtags like that?"

Dalia checked the video she'd originally seen about the berries. "Wow, I didn't realize how many hashtags Janeese uses." A few seconds later, she groaned. "There it is, #ad, but it was buried in a bunch of other ones."

"I bet she was hoping you wouldn't notice," said Nils. "If you know she's getting paid to promote something, then you're less likely to believe her claims, right?"

Dalia exited the app. "Now I feel even worse. I—wait a second." She opened the app, again. "Nils, look at this." Dalia turned the phone toward him.

CHAPTER TEN

THIS IS "BERRY" GOOD

"What am I looking at?" Nils asked.

"Janeese exaggerated what the berries could do because she was getting paid, but what about all of the comments from people who said that it worked for them?" asked Dalia. "I didn't see anyone saying the berries didn't help."

"Maybe they're lying to make Janeese like them," said Nils. "Have you tried posting that it didn't work?"

Dalia used her phone to post. **I tried eating the berries but nothing happened. Plus, I did some research and there's no proof they will make you grow fast.**

Nils read over her shoulder. "Hopefully, you'll find some answers now."

While they waited, Nils showed Dalia more of the videos he'd seen under the hashtag #cybersleuths.

"This one is about how to verify if an internet story is true," said Nils.

Dalia watched @cybersleuth14 talk about reputable sites and verifying sources. "Yeah, my mom said something like that. She helped me figure out that Janeese wasn't being a hundred percent honest." Dalia nudged Nils. "Like you did."

Dalia scrolled back to her comment to see if anyone had any suggestions. But she couldn't find it. "Hey—my comment disappeared."

Nils tilted his head. "Did it disappear, or did Janeese delete it?"

"She can do that?" asked Dalia.

"Sure. If she doesn't like what you're saying, she can delete the comment," said Nils.

"That's not right!" Dalia said. "That means that people might have had the same experience as me, but now I won't know."

"That also means other people won't know about your experience, either," said Nils.

"You know what else I need? A way to stop misinformation that people like Janeese keep sharing." She grinned. "And I think I have an idea."

Nils grinned back. "A video, like what @cybersleuth14 and @cybersleuthchyenne posted?"

"Exactly!" said Dalia. "We can add hashtags like #cybertruth and #cybersleuth so people can find other videos like ours."

Nils grabbed a pen and paper. "How do we want to do this?"

"I have to wear a mask," said Dalia. "I promised my parents I wouldn't have my face online. After that, we should talk about what Janeese's videos claim about the berries. Then we can link to the sites I used to prove her claims were false."

Nils nodded. "We should talk about the kinds of sites to use for verifying other videos, like universities or websites of scientific organizations."

"Then we can talk about what the berries can really do," said Dalia. "They're definitely great for you, but they're not magic."

Nils took a bite of the pie. "We should totally end the video with this recipe your dad used for this pie. It is magic that he turned sour berries into something this delicious!" Nils said as berry juice dribbled down his chin.

****

"Ready?" Nils adjusted the ring light and hit the power. He pointed the phone at her.

"Ready!" Dalia adjusted her mask. "Hi," she said into the phone. "Online, I go by the name @cybersleuthd, and I'm here to talk about a Clik-Clok trend that's full of misinformation. A lot of influencers are talking about aronia berries. They claim they can help people grow an inch or more in a week. I'm here to tell you why this isn't true. I'm also here to show you how you can verify online claims and make sure they're accurate." Dalia smiled. "Ready? Let's begin."

GLOSSARY

antioxidant (an-tee-OK-si-dant)—a molecule found naturally in the body that protects a person from free radicals

aronia berries (uh-ROH-nee-uh BEHR-eez)—small, dark fruits that resemble blueberries and have a sour taste that dries out the mouth; also called chokeberries

click (KLIK)—a unit of measurement designed to let account holders and social media designers know how popular a specific post, advertisement, or influencer is

follower (FOL-loh-er)—a social media member who tracks another person on the same app, providing support and learning about them and their interests from the content provided

free radical (FREE RAD-i-kuhl)—an unstable molecule in the body, which can build up in cells and cause damage to the body

like (LYK)—an emoticon, such as a heart or thumbs-up, that lets a social media account holder know who or how many approve of their posts

social media (SOH-shuhl MEE-dee-uh)—a type of digital technology that connects groups of individuals through an online network

superfruit (SOO-per-froot)—fruit that is said to have higher than normal nutritional benefits to the body

THE CYBER SLEUTHS CODE

Here is how you, as an expert cyber sleuth, can connect to the ISTE Student Standards.

BE AN EMPOWERED LEARNER
Cyber Sleuths use technology to set goals, work toward achieving them, and demonstrate their learning.

BE A DIGITAL CITIZEN
Cyber Sleuths understand the rights, responsibilities, and opportunities of living, learning, and working in an interconnected digital world.

BE A KNOWLEDGE CONSTRUCTOR
Cyber Sleuths critically select, evaluate, and synthesize digital resources into a collection that reflects their learning and builds their knowledge.

BE AN INNOVATIVE DESIGNER
Cyber Sleuths solve problems by creating new and imaginative solutions using a variety of digital tools.

BE A COMPUTATIONAL THINKER
Cyber Sleuths identify authentic problems, work with data, and use a step-by-step process to automate solutions.

BE A CREATIVE COMMUNICATOR
Cyber Sleuths communicate effectively and express themselves creatively using different tools, styles, formats, and digital media.

BE A GLOBAL COLLABORATOR
Cyber Sleuths strive to broaden their perspective, understand others, and work effectively in teams using digital tools.

RESOURCES

Be Internet Awesome
beinternetawesome.withgoogle.com/en_us

Common Sense Media
commonsense.org/education/digital-citizenship

International Society for Technology
in Education (ISTE)
iste.org

ABOUT THE AUTHOR

Natasha Deen graduated from college with a psychology degree, but her passion has always revolved around stories. She has written mysteries, action, historical, and fantasy novels for kids, teens, and adults. For her, one of the best things about being an author is the chance to slip into other times and worlds, and to be anything she can imagine through her characters. Natasha lives in Edmonton, Alberta, Canada, with her pets and husband. When she's not writing, she spends a lot of time trying to convince her animals that she's the real boss of the house. Visit her at www.natashadeen.com.

ABOUT THE ILLUSTRATOR

Mariano Epelbaum is a character designer, illustrator, and traditional 2D animator. He has been working professionally since 1996 in various disciplines of animation and illustration, where character designs tend to be very expressive and original. Currently, Mariano works as an art director on several projects. He is always trying different styles and techniques.